About *The Wind in the Willows*

In *The Wind in the Willows* Kenneth Grahame created a wonderful world inhabited by four memorable animal friends—Toad, Rat, Mole, and Badger. The book takes place in the early 1900's, against a backdrop of English river-bank, forest, and countryside. At that time, a new "animal" came onto the landscape—the automobile. Toad's fascination with cars and the trouble Toad gets into because of them have provided humorous entertainment for generations of readers.

The Wind in the Willows

By Kenneth Grahame

Illustrations by Susan Wheeler

Abridged Easy-to-Read Edition

Publishers • GROSSET & DUNLAP • *New York*

Grosset & Dunlap Junior Classics

Black Beauty
Heidi
The Swiss Family Robinson
The Wind in the Willows

These and many other exciting classics are
also available in deluxe, unabridged
Grosset & Dunlap Illustrated Junior Library® editions.

Contents

1

The River Bank

The Mole had been working hard all morning spring-cleaning his home. Suddenly he flung down his brush and bolted out of the house without even waiting to put on his coat. Something up above was calling him. He made for the steep little tunnel which led to the sun and air. He scraped and scratched, working busily with his little paws. At last, *pop!* his snout came out into the sunlight, and he found himself rolling in the warm grass of a great meadow.

"This is fine!" he said to himself. "This is better than whitewashing!" Jumping off all his four legs at once, in the joy of living and the delight of spring without its cleaning, he made his way across the meadow.

He thought his happiness was complete when, as he wandered along, suddenly he stood by the edge of a river. Never in his life had he seen a river before—all glints and gleams and sparkles, rustle and swirl, chatter and bubble. The Mole was bewitched, entranced, fascinated.

As he sat on the grass and looked across the river, a dark hole in the bank opposite, just above the water's edge, caught his eye. As he gazed, something bright and small seemed to twinkle down in the heart of it, vanished, then twinkled once more like a tiny star.

Then, as he looked, it winked at him, and so declared itself to be an eye. A small face began gradually to grow up around it, like a frame around a picture. A brown little face, with whiskers.

It was the Water Rat! The two animals stood and looked at each other cautiously.

"Hullo, Mole!" said the Water Rat.

"Hullo, Rat!" said the Mole.

"Would you like to come over?" inquired the Rat. He stooped and unfastened a rope and hauled on it. Then he stepped lightly into a little boat painted blue outside and w within, just the size for two animals.

The Rat sculled smartly across and made fast. Then he held up his forepaw as the Mole stepped gingerly down. "Lean on that!" he said. The Mole, to his surprise and rapture, found himself actually seated in the stern of a real boat.

Waggling his toes from sheer happiness, he spread his chest with a sigh of contentment and leaned back blissfully into the soft cushions. "*What* a day I'm having!" he said. "Let us start at once!"

The Rat pointed to a fat wicker luncheon basket. "Shove that under your feet," he said to the Mole. "It's what I always take along on these trips."

The Mole, absorbed in the new life he was entering upon—the sparkle, the ripple, the scents and the sounds and the sunlight—trailed a paw in the water and dreamed long waking dreams. The Water Rat, like the good little fellow he was, sculled steadily on and did not disturb him.

"I beg your pardon," said the Mole, pulling himself together at last. "You must think me very rude. But all this is so new to me. So—this—is—a—River!"

"Yes," said the Rat. "It's my world, and I don't want any other. What it hasn't got is not worth having, and what it doesn't know is not worth knowing. Whether in winter or summer, spring or autumn, it's always got its fun and its excitements.

"Of course, it isn't what it used to be. Otters, kingfishers, dabchicks, moorhens, all of them about all day long and always wanting you to *do* something—as if a fellow had no business of his own to attend to!"

The Rat brought the boat alongside the bank and made it fast. He helped the still awkward Mole safely ashore and swung out the luncheon basket.

The Mole begged as a favor to be allowed to unpack it all by himself. The Rat was very pleased to sprawl out on the grass and rest while his excited friend shook out the tablecloth and spread it, took out all the mysterious packets one by one and arranged their contents, gasping, "Oh, my! Oh, my!" each time.

When all was ready, the Rat said, "Now,

pitch in, old fellow!" The Mole was very glad to obey.

A broad glistening muzzle showed itself above the edge of the bank, and the Otter came out and shook the water from his coat.

"Greedy beggars!" he observed, glancing at the food. "Why didn't you invite me, Ratty?"

"This was not a planned affair," explained the Rat. "By the way—my friend, Mr. Mole."

"Proud, I'm sure," said the Otter, and the two animals were friends at once.

"Such a rumpus everywhere!" continued the Otter. "All the world seems out on the river today. I can't get a moment's peace. Toad's out, for one, in his brand-new wager-boat. New togs, new everything!"

"Once, it was nothing but sailing," said the Rat. "Then he tired of that and took to punting. Nothing would please him but to punt all day and every day, and a nice mess he made of it. Last year it was houseboating, and we all had to go and stay with him in his houseboat, and pretend we liked it."

A stray May fly swerved unsteadily across the current near the surface. A swirl of water and a *cloop!* and the May fly was visible no more.

Neither was the Otter.

The Rat hummed a tune, and the Mole remembered that animal etiquette forbade any sort of comment on the sudden disappearance of one's friends at any moment, for any reason or no reason whatever.

"Well, well," said the Rat, "I suppose we ought to be moving. I wonder which of us had better pack the luncheon basket?" He did not speak as if he was eager to do so.

"Oh, please let me," said the Mole. So, of course, the Rat let him.

The afternoon sun was getting low as the Rat sculled gently homeward in a dreamy mood, murmuring poetry-things over to himself, and not paying much attention to Mole. But the Mole was very full of lunch, and self-satisfaction, and pride, and already quite at home in a boat (so he thought) and was getting restless, besides. He said, "Ratty! Please, *I* want to row now!"

The Rat shook his head with a smile. "Not yet, my young friend," he said. "Wait till you've had a few lessons. It's not so easy as it looks. I really think you had better come and stop with me for a little time. I'll teach you to row, and to swim, and you'll soon be as handy on the water as any of us."

The Mole was so touched by this kind manner of speaking that he could find no voice to answer him, and he had to brush away a tear or two with the back of his paw.

When they got home, the Rat made a bright fire in the parlor, and planted the Mole in an armchair in front of it, having fetched down a dressing gown and slippers for him. Then the Rat told river stories till suppertime.

Supper was a cheerful meal. But very shortly a terribly sleepy Mole had to be led upstairs to the best bedroom, where he soon laid his head on his pillow in great peace and contentment, knowing that his new-found friend the River was lapping the sill of his window.

2

The Open Road

"Ratty," said the Mole suddenly one bright summer morning, "if you please, I want to ask you a favor."

The Rat was sitting on the river bank, singing a little song which he had just made up about his friends the ducks, which he called:

Ducks' Ditty

All along the backwater,
Through the rushes tall,
Ducks are a-dabbling,
Up tails all!

Ducks' tails, drakes' tails,
Yellow feet a-quiver,
Yellow bills all out of sight
Busy in the river!

Slushy green undergrowth
Where the roach swim—
Here we keep our larder,
Cool and full and dim.

Everyone for what he likes!
We like to be
Heads down, tails up,
Dabbling free!

High in the blue above
Swifts whirl and call—
We are down a-dabbling,
Up tails all!

"I don't know that I think so *very* much of that little song, Rat," observed the Mole cautiously. "But what I wanted to ask you was, won't you take me to call on Mr. Toad? I've heard so much about him."

"Why, certainly," said the good-natured Rat, jumping to his feet. "Get the boat out, and we'll paddle up there at once."

"Toad must be a very nice animal," observed the Mole as he got in the boat and took the sculls. Rat settled himself comfortably in the stern.

"Toad is indeed the best of animals," replied Rat. "So simple, so good-natured, and so affectionate. Perhaps he's not very clever, but he has other good qualities."

Rounding a bend in the river, they saw a handsome, dignified old house of mellowed red brick with well-kept lawns reaching down to the water's edge.

"There's Toad Hall," said the Rat. "Toad is rather rich, you know, and this is really one of the nicest houses in these parts."

They glided up the creek, went ashore and strolled across the gay flower-decked lawns in search of Toad. They soon found him sitting in a wicker garden chair, a large map spread out on his knees.

"Hooray!" he cried, jumping up on seeing them. "This is splendid!" He shook the paws of both of them warmly, never waiting for an introduction to the Mole. "You don't know how lucky it is, your turning up just now!"

"It's about your rowing, I suppose," said the Rat, with an innocent air.

"Oh, pooh! Boating!" interrupted the Toad. "Silly boyish amusement. I've given that up *long* ago. Sheer waste of time, that's what it is. No, I've discovered the real thing, the only

genuine occupation for a lifetime. Come with me, dear Ratty, and your amiable friend also, if he will be so good."

He led the way to the stableyard, the Rat following with a mistrustful expression, and there they saw a gypsy caravan, shining with newness, painted yellow, with red wheels.

"There you are!" cried the Toad. "There's real life for you, right in that little cart. The open road, the dusty highway, the hedgerows! Camps, villages, towns, cities! Here today, and off tomorrow! Travel, change, interest, excitement! The whole world before you, and a horizon that's always changing! And this is the very finest cart of its sort that was ever built. Come inside and look at the arrangements. Planned 'em all myself, I did!"

It was indeed very compact and comfortable. Little sleeping bunks, a table that folded up against the wall, a cooking-stove, lockers, bookshelves, a birdcage with a bird in it; and pots, pans, and kettles of every size.

"All complete!" said the Toad triumphantly, pulling open a locker. "You see— biscuits, potted lobster, sardines—everything you can possibly want. Soda water, letter paper, bacon, jam, cards, and dominoes. You'll find," he continued as they descended the steps again, "that nothing whatever has been forgotten, when we make our start this afternoon."

"I beg your pardon," said the Rat slowly, as he chewed a straw, "but did I overhear you say something about *'we'* and *'start'* and *'this afternoon'*?"

"Now, don't begin talking in that stiff and sniffy way, because you know you've *got* to come," said Toad. "I can't possibly manage without you, so please consider it settled, and don't argue. You surely don't mean to stick to your dull old river all your life, and just live in a hole in a bank, and *boat*? I want to show you the world! I'm going to make an *animal* of you, my boy!"

During luncheon—which was excellent, of course, as everything at Toad Hall always was—the Toad painted the prospects of the trip and the joys of the open road in glowing colors. Somehow, it soon seemed taken for granted by all three of them that the trip was a settled thing.

When they were quite ready, the Toad led his companions to the paddock. An old gray horse was harnessed, and they set off, all talking at once. It was a golden afternoon. The smell of the dust they kicked up was rich and satisfying. Birds called and whistled to them cheerily. Good-natured wayfarers passing them gave them "Good day," or stopped to say nice things about their beautiful cart. And rabbits, sitting at their front doors in the hedgerows, held up their forepaws, and said, "Oh, my! Oh, my! Oh, my!"

Late in the evening, tired and happy and miles from home, they turned the horse loose to graze, and ate a simple supper sitting by the side of the cart, while stars grew fuller and larger all around them. At last they turned into their little bunks in the cart. And Toad, kicking out his legs, sleepily said, "Well, good night, fellows! This is the real life for a gentleman!"

They had a pleasant ramble next day over grassy downs and along narrow by-lanes, and it was not till the afternoon that they came out on their first highroad.

They were moving along easily, when far

behind them they heard a faint warning hum, like the drone of a distant bee. Glancing back, they saw a small cloud of dust advancing on them at incredible speed, while from out the dust a faint "Poop-poop!" wailed like an uneasy animal in pain.

In an instant the peaceful scene was changed. With a blast of wind and a whirl of sound that made them jump, it was on them! The magnificent motorcar, immense and breath-snatching, with its driver tense and hugging his wheel, flung a cloud of dust that blinded and enveloped them. Then it dwindled to a speck in the far distance, changed back into a droning bee once more.

The old gray horse simply abandoned himself to his natural emotions. Rearing, plunging, he drove the cart backward toward the deep ditch at the side of the road. It wavered an instant. Then there was a heartrending crash, and the yellow cart lay on its side in the ditch.

The Toad sat straight down in the middle of the dusty road, his legs stretched out before him, and stared fixedly in the direction of the disappearing motorcar. He breathed short, his face wore a placid, satisfied expression, and at intervals he faintly murmured, "Poop-poop!"

The Rat shook him by the shoulder. "Are you coming to help us, Toad?" he demanded sternly.

"Glorious, stirring sight!" murmured Toad, never offering to move. "The poetry of motion! The *real* way to travel! The *only* way to travel! Villages skipped, towns and cities jumped—always somebody else's horizon! Oh, bliss! Oh, poop-poop! Oh, my! Oh, my!"

"What are we to do with him?" asked the Mole of the Water Rat.

"Nothing at all," replied the Rat firmly. "Because there is really nothing to be done. You see, I know him from old. When he has a new craze, it always takes him that way, in its first stage. He'll continue like that for days now, quite useless for all practical purposes. Never mind him. It's five or six miles to the nearest town, and we must walk it. The sooner we start the better."

"But what about Toad?" asked the Mole anxiously, as they set off together.

"Oh, *bother* Toad," said the Rat savagely. "I've done with him!"

They had not gone very far, however, when there was a pattering of feet behind them. Toad caught them up and thrust a paw inside the elbow of each of them.

"Oh, Ratty!" he gasped. "You can't think how obliged I am to you for consenting to come on this trip! I wouldn't have gone without you, and then I might never have seen that—that swan, that sunbeam, that thunderbolt! I might never have heard that entrancing sound, or smelled that bewitching smell! I owe it all to you, my best of friends!"

The Rat turned from him in despair. "You see?" he said to the Mole. "He's quite hopeless. I give it up. When we get to the town we'll go to the railway station, and with luck we may get a train there that'll get us back to River Bank tonight."

On reaching the town they went straight to the station. Eventually, a slow train landed them not very far from Toad Hall. They got out their boat, sculled down the river home, and at a very late hour sat down to supper.

The following evening the Mole, who had risen late and taken things very easy all day, was sitting on the bank fishing. The Rat, who had been looking up his friends and gossiping, came strolling along to find him. "Heard the news?" he said. "It's the talk of the river bank. Toad went up to town by an early train this morning. He has ordered a large and very expensive motorcar."

3

The Wild Wood

The Mole had long wanted to make the acquaintance of the Badger. But whenever the Mole mentioned his wish to the Water Rat, he always found himself put off. "It's all right," the Rat would say, "Badger'll turn up some day or other—he's always turning up—and then I'll introduce you."

The Mole had to be content with this. But the Badger never came along, and every day brought its amusements. It was not till summer was long over, and cold and frost and miry ways kept them much indoors, that Mole again thought of the solitary, gray Badger, who lived his own life by himself.

One afternoon, when the Rat in his armchair before the fire was alternately dozing and trying over rhymes that wouldn't fit, the Mole decided to go out by himself and explore the Wild Wood, and perhaps meet Mr. Badger.

It was a cold, still afternoon with a hard steely sky overhead, when he slipped out of the warm parlor into the open air, pushing on cheerfully.

There was nothing to alarm him at first. Twigs crackled under his feet, logs tripped him, but that was all fun, and exciting. It led him on, and he penetrated to where the light was less and trees crouched nearer and nearer.

Then the faces began.

It was over his shoulder, and indistinctly, that he first thought he saw a little evil wedge-shaped face, looking out at him from a hole. When he turned, the thing had vanished.

He quickened his pace, telling himself not to begin imagining things, or there would be no end to it. Then suddenly, as if it had been so all the time, every hole, far and near, seemed to have a face, coming and going rapidly.

If he could only get away from the holes in

the banks, he thought, there would be no more faces. He swung off the path and plunged into the wood.

Then the whistling began.

Very faint and shrill it was, and far behind him, when he first heard it. But somehow it made him hurry forward. Then, still very faint and shrill, it sounded far ahead of him, and made him hesitate and want to go back. They were up and alert and ready, evidently, who-ever they were! And he—he was alone, and unarmed, and far from any help. The night was closing in.

Then the pattering began.

He thought it was only falling leaves at first, so slight and delicate was the sound of it. Then the pattering increased till it sounded like sudden hail on the dry-leaf carpet spread around him. The whole wood seemed running now, running hard, hunting, chasing, closing in round something or—somebody?

In panic, he began to run too, aimlessly. He ran up against things, he fell over things and into things, he darted under things and dodged round things. At last he crawled into the deep dark hollow of an old beech tree, which offered shelter, concealment—perhaps even safety. Anyhow, he was too tired to run any farther and could only snuggle down into some dry leaves.

As he lay there panting and trembling, and listened to the whistlings and the patterings outside, he knew at last, in all its fullness, that dread thing which the Rat had tried to shield him from—the Terror of the Wild Wood!

Meantime the Rat, warm and comfortable, dozed by his fireside. Then a coal slipped, and he woke with a start.

"Moly!" he called several times, and, receiving no answer, got up and went out into the hall.

The Mole's cap was missing from its peg. His galoshes, which always lay by the umbrella stand, were also gone.

The Rat left the house and carefully examined the muddy surface of the ground outside, hoping to find the Mole's tracks. There they were, sure enough, leading direct to the Wild Wood.

The Rat stood in deep thought for a minute or two. Then he reentered the house and strapped a belt around his waist. He shoved two pistols into it, took up a stout cudgel, and quickly set off for the Wild Wood.

It was already almost dusk when he plunged without hesitation into the wood, looking anxiously for any sign of his friend, all the time calling out cheerfully, "Moly, Moly, Moly! Where are you? It's me—Rat!"

He had hunted through the wood for an hour or more, when at last he heard a little answering cry. Guiding himself by the sound, he made his way to the foot of an old beech tree, and from out of the hole in it came a feeble voice, saying, "Ratty! Is that really you?"

The Rat crept into the hollow, and there he found the Mole, exhausted and still trembling. "Oh, Rat!" he cried, "I've been so frightened!"

"Oh, I quite understand," said the Rat soothingly. "Now then, we really must pull ourselves together and make a start for home while there's still a little light left. It will never do to spend the night here, you understand."

"Why? What's up, Ratty?" asked the Mole.

"*Snow* is up," replied the Rat briefly, "or rather, *down*. It's snowing hard. We must make a start, and take our chance, I suppose.

The worst of it is, I don't exactly know where we are. And now this snow makes everything look so very different."

It did indeed. The Mole would not have known that it was the same wood. However, they set out bravely, pretending that they recognized an old friend in every fresh tree that grimly and silently greeted them.

An hour or two later they sat down on a fallen tree trunk to recover their breath. They had fallen into several holes and got wet through. The snow was getting so deep that they could hardly drag their little legs through it, and the trees were thicker than ever. There seemed to be no end to this wood, and no beginning, and no difference in it, and—worst of all—no way out.

"We can't sit here very long," said the Rat. "We shall have to make another push for it, and do something or other. The cold is too awful for anything, and the snow will soon be too deep for us to wade through."

Once more they got on their feet, but suddenly the Mole tripped up and fell forward on his face with a squeal.

"Oh, my leg!" he cried. "Oh, my poor

shin!" and he sat up on the snow and nursed his leg in both his front paws.

"Poor old Mole!" said the Rat kindly. "You don't seem to be having much luck today, do you? Let's have a look at the leg. Yes," he went on, going down on his knees to look, "you've cut your shin, sure enough. That was never done by a branch or a stump. Looks as if it was made by a sharp edge of something in metal."

"Well, never mind what done it," said the Mole, forgetting his grammar in his pain. "It hurts just the same, whatever done it."

Some ten minutes' hard work, and the point of the Rat's cudgel struck something that sounded hollow. He worked till he could get a paw through and feel, then called to Mole to come and help him. Hard at it went the two animals, till at last the result of their labors was in full view.

In the side of what had seemed to be a snowbank stood a solid-looking, little door painted a dark green. An iron bellpull hung by the side, and below it, on a small brass plate, they could read by the aid of moonlight: MR. BADGER.

The Mole fell backward on the snow from sheer surprise and delight. "Rat," he cried, "you're a wonder! A real wonder, that's what you are!"

While the Rat attacked the door with his stick, the Mole sprang up at the bellpull. He clutched it and swung there, both feet well off the ground. From quite a long way off they could faintly hear a deep-toned bell.

They waited patiently for what seemed a very long time, stamping in the snow to keep their feet warm. At last they heard the sound of slow shuffling footsteps approaching the door from the inside.

There was the noise of a bolt shot back, and the door opened a few inches, enough to show a long snout and a pair of sleepy blinking eyes.

"Oh, Badger," cried the Rat, "let us in, please. It's me—Rat—and my friend Mole, and we've lost our way in the snow."

"What, Ratty, my dear little man!" exclaimed the Badger. "Come in, both of you, at once. Well, I never! Lost in the snow! And in the Wild Wood, too, and at this time of night! But come in with you."

The two animals tumbled over each other in their eagerness to get inside, and soon found themselves amid the warmth of a large fire-lit kitchen.

The kindly Badger thrust them down to toast themselves at the fire, and bade them remove their wet coats and boots. Then he fetched them dressing gowns and slippers, and he bathed the Mole's shin with warm water and bandaged the cut till the whole thing was just as good as new, if not better.

When at last they were thoroughly toasted, the Badger called them to the table to dine. Conversation was impossible for a long time. When it was slowly resumed, it was the sort of conversation that results from talking with your mouth full.

When supper was finished at last, and after they had chatted for a time about things in general, the Badger said heartily, "Now, then! Tell us the news from your part of the world. How's old Toad going on?"

"Oh, from bad to worse," said the Rat gravely. "Another smashup only last week, a bad one. But he's convinced he's a heaven-

born driver, and nobody can teach him anything."

"How many has he had?" inquired the
Badger gloomily.

"Smashes, or machines?" asked the Rat.
"Oh, well, after all, it's the same thing—with
Toad. This is the seventh."

"He's been in hospital three times," put in
the Mole, "and as for the fines he's had to
pay, it's simply awful to think of."

"Yes, and that's part of the trouble," continued the Rat. "Killed or ruined—it's got to
be one of the two things, sooner or later.
Badger, we're his friends! Oughtn't we to do
something?"

The Badger went through a bit of hard
thinking. "Now, look here," he said at last,
rather severely, "of course you know I can't
do anything *now*?"

His two friends agreed, quite understand-
ing his point. No animal, according to the
rules of animal etiquette, is ever expected to
do anything strenuous, or heroic, or even
moderately active during the winter. All are
sleepy—some actually asleep.

"Very well, then!" continued the Badger.

"*But*, when once the year has really turned, and the nights are shorter, we'll take Toad seriously in hand. We'll stand no nonsense whatever. We'll bring him back to reason. We'll *make* him be a sensible Toad."

4

Homecoming

The Mole and the Water Rat, in high spirits, were returning across country after a long day's outing with Otter, hunting and exploring on the wide uplands where streams had their first small beginnings. The shades of the short winter day were closing in on them.

They plodded along steadily, each of them thinking his own thoughts. The Mole's ran a good deal on supper, as it was pitch-dark. This was all a strange country to him as far as he knew, and he was following obediently in the wake of the Rat, leaving the guidance entirely to him.

As for the Rat, he was walking a little way ahead, his shoulders humped, his eyes fixed on the road in front of him. He did not notice when a mysterious call suddenly reached Mole in the darkness, making him tingle through and through. He stopped dead in his tracks, his nose searching hither and thither in its efforts to recapture something.

Home! That was what they meant, those caressing appeals, those soft touches wafting through the air, those invisible little hands pulling and tugging, all one way! Why, it must be quite close by him at that moment, his old home that he had hurriedly forsaken and never sought again, that day when he first found the river! And now, with a rush of old memories, how clearly it stood up before him, in the darkness!

Shabby indeed, and small and poorly furnished, and yet his, the home he had made for himself, the home he had been so happy to get back to after his day's work. And the home had been happy with him, too, evidently, and was missing him, and was telling him so, through his nose, reminding him that it was there, and wanted him.

The call was clear, the summons was plain.

He must obey it instantly, and go. "Ratty," he called, full of joyful excitement, "hold on! Come back! I want you, quick!"

"Mole, we mustn't stop now, really!" the Rat called back. "We'll come for it tomorrow, whatever it is you've found. But I daren't stop now—it's late, and the snow's coming on again, and I'm not sure of the way! And I want your nose, Mole, so come on quick, there's a good fellow!" And the Rat pressed forward on his way without waiting for an answer.

Poor Mole stood alone in the road, his heart torn apart, and a big sob gathering, gathering, somewhere low down inside him. Up and up, it forced its way to the air. Then another, and another, and others thick and fast. Poor Mole at last gave up the struggle and cried freely and helplessly and openly, now that he knew it was all over and he had lost what he could hardly be said to have found.

The Rat, astonished and dismayed at the Mole's grief, did not dare to speak for a while. At last he said, very quietly and sympathetically, "What is it, old fellow? Whatever can be the matter?"

Poor Mole found it difficult to get any words out. "I know it's a—shabby, dingy little place," he sobbed forth at last, brokenly: "not like—your cozy quarters—or Toad's beautiful hall—or Badger's great house—but it was my own little home—and I was fond of it—and I went away and forgot all about it—and then I smelled it suddenly—on the road, when I called and everything came back to me with a rush—and I *wanted* it!—Oh, dear! Oh, dear!"

Recollection brought fresh waves of sorrow, and sobs again took full charge of him, preventing further speech.

The Rat stared straight in front of him, saying nothing, only patting Mole gently on the shoulder. He waited till Mole's sobs became gradually less stormy. Then he rose from his seat and, remarking carelessly, "Well, now we'd really better be getting on, old chap!" set off up the road again, over the way they had come.

"Wherever are you—*hic* going to—*hic*, Ratty?" cried the tearful Mole, looking up in alarm.

"We're going to find that home of yours, old fellow," replied the Rat pleasantly, "so you had better come along, for it will take some finding, and we shall want your nose."

Mole stood a moment rigid, while his up-lifted nose, quivering slightly, felt the air. Then a short, quick run forward—a fault—a check—a try back. Then a slow, steady, confident advance.

The Rat, much excited, kept close to his heels. The Mole, with something of the air of a sleepwalker, crossed a dry ditch, scrambled through a hedge, and nosed his way over a field open and trackless and bare in the faint starlight.

Suddenly, without warning, he dived. But the Rat was on the alert and promptly followed the Mole down the tunnel to which his unerring nose had faithfully led him.

It was close and airless, and the earthy smell was strong. It seemed a long time to Rat before the passage ended and he could stand erect and stretch and shake himself. The Mole struck a match, and by its light the Rat saw that they were standing in an open space neatly swept and sanded underfoot. Directly facing them was Mole's little front door, with MOLE END painted over the bellpull at the side.

The Mole reached down a lantern from a nail on the wall and lit it. He hurried Rat through the door, lit a lamp in the hall, and took one glance around his old home. He saw the dust lying thick on everything, saw the cheerless, deserted look of the long-neglected house, and its worn and shabby contents—and collapsed again on a hall chair.

"Oh, Ratty!" he cried dismally. "Why ever did I bring you to this poor, cold little place, on a night like this, when you might have been at River Bank by this time, with all your own nice things about you!"

The Rat, however, was running here and there, opening doors, inspecting rooms and cupboards, and lighting lamps and candles. "What a capital little house this is!" he called out cheerily. "So compact! So well planned! Everything here and everything in its place! We'll make a jolly night of it. The first thing we want is a good fire. I'll fetch the wood and the coals, and you get a duster, Mole, and try and smarten things up a bit."

Encouraged by his companion, the Mole roused himself and dusted and polished, while the Rat, running to and fro with armfuls of fuel, soon had a cheerful blaze roaring. He hailed the Mole to come and warm himself. But suddenly sounds were heard from the forecourt—sounds like the scuffling of small feet in the gravel and a confused murmur of tiny voices.

"What's up?" inquired the Rat, pausing in his labors.

"I think it must be the field mice," replied the Mole, with a touch of pride in his manner. "They go round carol-singing regularly at this time of the year. They're quite an institution in these parts."

"Let's have a look at them!" cried the Rat, jumping up and running to the door to fling it open.

In the forecourt, lit by the dim rays of a lantern, some eight or ten little field mice stood in a semicircle, red scarfs around their throats, their forepaws thrust deep into their pockets, their feet jiggling for warmth. With bright beady eyes they glanced shyly at each other, sniggering a little, sniffing and applying coat sleeves a good deal.

As the door opened, one of the elder ones that carried the lantern was just saying, "Now then, one, two, three!" and forthwith their shrill little voices sang an old-time carol.

"Very well sung, boys!" cried the Rat heartily. "And now come along in, all of you, and warm yourselves by the fire."

"Oh, Ratty!" cried the Mole in despair, plumping down on a seat, with tears impending. "We have nothing to give them!"

"You leave all that to me," said the masterful Rat. "Here, you with the lantern! Come over this way. Tell me, are there any shops open at this hour of the night?"

"Why, certainly, sir," replied the field mouse respectfully. "At this time of the year our shops keep open to all sorts of hours."

"Then look here! said the Rat. "You go off at once, and you get me . . ."

Here much muttered conversation ensued. Finally, there was a chink of coin passing from paw to paw, the field mouse was provided with a basket for his purchases, and off he hurried. The rest of the field mice gave themselves up to enjoyment of the fire.

Soon the field mouse with the lantern reappeared, staggering under the weight of his basket. Under the generalship of Rat, every-

body was set to do something or to fetch something. In a very few minutes supper was ready, and Mole took his place at the head of the table, thinking what a happy homecoming this had turned out, after all.

5

Mr. Toad

It was a bright morning in the early part of summer. The Mole and the Water Rat were finishing breakfast in their little parlor, when a heavy knock sounded at the door.

The Badger strode heavily into the room, and stood looking at the two animals with an expression full of seriousness. The Rat let his egg spoon fall on the tablecloth, and sat open-mouthed.

"The hour has come!" said the Badger at last with great solemnity.

"What hour?" asked the Rat uneasily, glancing at the clock.

"*Whose* hour, you should say," replied the Badger. "Why, Toad's hour! I said I would take him in hand as soon as the winter was well over, and I'm going to take him in hand today!"

"Toad's hour, of course!" cried the Mole delightedly. "I remember now! *We'll* teach him to be a sensible Toad!"

"This very morning," continued the Badger, taking an armchair, "another new and exceptionally powerful motorcar will arrive at Toad Hall on approval or return. We must be up and doing, before it is too late. Off to Toad Hall! The work of rescue shall be accomplished."

"Right you are!" cried the Rat. "We'll rescue the poor, unhappy animal! We'll convert him! He'll be the most converted Toad that ever was before we've done with him!"

They set off up the road, Badger leading the way, and reached the carriage drive of Toad Hall to find, as the Badger had anticipated, a shiny new motorcar, painted a bright red (Toad's favorite color), in front of the house.

As they neared the door, it was flung open, and Mr. Toad, in goggles, cap, gaiters, and enormous overcoat, came swaggering down the steps, drawing on his gloves.

"Hullo! Come on, you fellows!" he cried cheerfully on catching sight of them. "You're just in time to come with me for a jolly—to come for a jolly—for a—er—jolly—"

His words faltered and fell away as he noticed the stern, unbending look on the faces of his silent friends.

The Badger strode up the steps. "Take him inside," he said sternly to his companions. Then, as Toad was hustled through the door struggling and protesting, he turned to the chauffeur in charge of the new motorcar.

"I'm afraid you won't be wanted today," he said. "Mr. Toad has changed his mind. He will not require the car. Please understand that this is final. You needn't wait." Then he followed the others inside and shut the door.

"Now, then!" he said to the Toad, when the four of them stood together in the hall, "first of all, take those ridiculous things off!"

"Shan't!" replied Toad. "What is the meaning of this? I demand an instant explanation."

"Take them off him, then, you two," ordered the Badger briefly.

They had to lay Toad out on the floor, kicking and calling all sorts of names, before they could get to work properly. Then the Rat sat on him, and the Mole got his motor clothes off him bit by bit, and they stood him up on his legs again.

"You knew it had to come to this, sooner or later, Toad," the Badger explained severely. "You've disregarded all the warnings we've given you, you've gone on squandering the money your father left you, and you're getting us animals a bad name by your furious driving and your smashes. We never allow our friends to make fools of themselves beyond a certain limit: and that limit you've reached.

"Now, you're a good fellow in many respects, and I don't want to be too hard on you. I'll make one more effort to bring you to reason."

He took Toad firmly by the arm, led him into the smoking room, and closed the door behind them.

"*That's* no good!" said the Rat. "Talking to Toad'll never cure him. He'll *say* anything."

After some three-quarters of an hour the door opened, and the Badger reappeared, solemnly leading by the paw a very limp and dejected Toad. His skin hung baggily about him—and his legs wobbled.

"Sit down there, Toad," said the Badger kindly, pointing to a chair. "My friends," he went on, "I am pleased to inform you that Toad has at last seen the error of his ways. He is truly sorry for his misguided conduct in the past, and he has undertaken to give up motorcars entirely and forever. I have his solemn promise to that effect."

"That is very good news," said the Mole gravely.

"Very good news, indeed," observed the Rat, "if only—*if* only——"

There was a long, long pause. Toad looked desperately this way and that, while the other animals waited in grave silence. At last he spoke.

"No!" he said a little sullenly, but stoutly, "I'm *not* sorry. And it wasn't folly at all! It was simply glorious!"

"What?" cried the Badger, greatly scandalized. "You backsliding animal, didn't you tell me just now, in there——"

"Oh, yes, yes, in *there*," said Toad impatiently. "I'd have said anything in *there*. You're so moving, and so convincing, and put all your points so frightfully well—you can do what you like with me in *there*, and you know it. But I find that I'm not a bit sorry, really, so it's no earthly good saying I am, now, is it?"

"Then you don't promise," said the Badger, "never to touch a motorcar again?"

"Certainly not!" replied Toad emphatically. "On the contrary, I faithfully promise that the very first motorcar I see, *poop-poop!* Off I go in it!"

"Told you so, didn't I?" observed the Rat to the Mole.

"Very well, then," said the Badger firmly, rising to his feet. "I feared it would come to this all along. You've often asked us three to come and stay with you, Toad. Well, now we're going to. Take him upstairs, you two, and lock him in his bedroom while we arrange matters between ourselves."

"It's for your own good, Toady, you know," said the Rat kindly, as Toad, kicking and struggling, was hauled up the stairs.

"Think what fun we shall have together, just as we used to, when you've quite got over this painful attack of yours!"

"We'll take great care of everything for you till you're well, Toad," said the Mole. "And we'll see your money isn't wasted, as it has been."

"No more incidents with the police, Toad," said the Rat, as they thrust him into his bedroom.

"And no more weeks in hospital," added the Mole, turning the key.

They descended the stair, Toad shouting abuse at them through the keyhole, and the three friends then met to discuss the situation.

"It's going to be a tedious business," said the Badger, sighing. "I've never seen Toad so determined. However, we will see it out. We shall have to take turns to be with him, till the poison has worked itself out of his system."

They arranged watches accordingly. Each animal took it in turns to sleep in Toad's room at night, and they divided the day up between them.

One fine morning the Rat went upstairs to relieve Badger, whom he found fidgeting to be off and stretch his legs in a long ramble. "Toad's still in bed," he told the Rat, outside the door. "Now, you look out, Rat! When Toad's quiet and submissive, there's sure to be something up. I know him. Well, now I must be off."

"How are you today, old chap?" inquired the Rat cheerfully as he approached Toad's bedside.

He had to wait some minutes for an answer. At last a feeble voice replied, "Thank you so much, dear Ratty! So good of you to inquire! But first tell me how you are yourself, and the excellent Mole?"

"Oh, *we're* all right," replied the Rat. "Mole," he added incautiously, "is going out for a run round with Badger. They'll be out till luncheontime, so I'll do my best to amuse you. Now jump up, there's a good fellow, and don't lie moping there."

"Dear, kind Rat," murmured Toad, "how very far I am from 'jumping up' now—if ever! But do not trouble about me. I hate being a burden to my friends, and I do not expect to be one much longer. Indeed, I almost hope not."

"Well, I hope not, too," said the Rat heartily. "You've been a fine bother to us all this time, and I'm glad to hear it's going to stop. It isn't the trouble we mind, but you're making us miss such an awful lot."

"I'm afraid it *is* the trouble you mind, though," replied the Toad languidly. "You're tired of bothering about me. I'm a nuisance, I know."

"You are, indeed," said the Rat. "But I tell you, I'd take any trouble on earth for you, if only you'd be a sensible animal."

"If I thought that, Ratty," murmured Toad, more feebly than ever, "then I would beg you—for the last time, probably—to fetch the doctor. But don't you bother. It's only a trouble, and perhaps we may as well let things take their course."

"Why, what do you want a doctor for?" inquired the Rat, coming closer and examining him. He certainly lay very still and flat, and his voice was weaker and his manner much changed.

"Surely you have noticed of late—" murmured Toad. "But no—why should you? Noticing things is only a trouble. Tomorrow, indeed, you may be saying to yourself, 'Oh, if only I had noticed sooner! If only I had done something!' But no; it's a trouble. Never mind—forget that I asked."

"Look here, old man," said the Rat, beginning to get rather alarmed, "of course I'll fetch a doctor to you, if you really think you want him." He hurried from the room, not forgetting, however, to lock the door carefully behind him, and then ran off to the village on his errand of mercy.

The Toad, who had hopped lightly out of bed as soon as he heard the key turned in the lock, watched him eagerly from the window till he disappeared down the carriage drive. Then he dressed as quickly as possible and filled his pockets with cash which he took from a small drawer in the dressing table.

Next, knotting the sheets from his bed together and tying one end fast, he scrambled out the window of his bedroom, slid lightly to the ground, and marched off, whistling a merry tune.

At first he took bypaths, and crossed many fields, and changed his course several times, in case of pursuit. But now, feeling safe, and the sun smiling brightly on him, he almost danced along the road in his satisfaction and conceit.

He strode along, his head in the air, till he reached a little town, where the sign of "The Red Lion" reminded him that he had not breakfasted that day. He marched into the inn and ordered the best luncheon that could be provided.

He was about halfway through his meal when a familiar sound drew nearer and nearer. The car turned into the inn yard, and Toad had to hold on to the leg of the table to conceal his excitement. Presently the party entered the room—hungry, talkative, and gay.

Toad at last could stand it no longer. He slipped out of the room quietly, paid his bill, and moved outside to the inn yard. "There cannot be any harm," he said to himself, "in my only *looking* at it!"

The car stood in the middle of the yard, quite unattended. Toad walked slowly round it, inspecting, criticizing, musing deeply.

"I wonder," he said to himself presently, "I wonder if this sort of car *starts* easily?"

Next moment, hardly knowing how it came

about, he found himself, somehow, seated in the driver's seat. As if in a dream, he drove the car round the yard and out through the archway.

Then he increased his speed, and as the car moved forth on the highroad through the open country, he was only conscious that he was Toad once more, Toad at his best and highest, Toad the Lord of the lone trail, before whom all must give way.

"To my mind," observed the Chairman of the Bench of Magistrates cheerfully, "the *only* difficulty that presents itself is how we can possibly make it sufficiently hot for the ruffian whom we see cowering before us. Let me see: he has been found guilty, on the clearest evidence, first, of stealing a valuable motorcar; secondly, of driving to the public danger; and, thirdly, of gross impertinence to the police.

"Mr. Clerk, will you tell us, please, what penalty we can impose for each of those offenses? Without, of course, giving the prisoner the benefit of any doubt, because there isn't any."

The Clerk scratched his nose with his pen.

"Judging by what we've heard from the witness box, even if you only believe one-tenth part of what you heard—and I never believe more myself—the penalties, if added together correctly, come to nineteen years——"

"First-rate!" said the Chairman.

"——So you had better make it a round twenty years and be on the safe side," concluded the Clerk.

"An excellent suggestion!" said the Chairman approvingly. "Prisoner! Pull yourself together and try and stand up straight. It's going to be twenty years for you this time. And mind, if you appear before us again, upon any charge whatever, we shall have to deal with you very seriously!"

The hapless Toad, loaded with chains, was dragged from the Courthouse, shrieking, praying, protesting; across the marketplace, past hooting school children; across the hollow-sounding drawbridge, under the frowning archway of the grim old castle; past guardrooms and sentries; up timeworn winding stairs; across courtyards, where mastiffs strained at their leashes and pawed the air to get at him; on, past the rack-chamber and the thumbscrew room, past the private scaffold, till they reached the door of the grimmest dungeon.

The rusty key creaked in the lock, and the great door clanged shut. Toad was a helpless prisoner in the stoutest castle in Merry England.

6

Toad's Adventures

When Toad found himself in this dank and noisome dungeon, he flung himself at full length on the floor, and shed bitter tears, and abandoned himself to dark despair. "This is the end of everything," he said. "Now I must languish in this dungeon, till people who were proud to say they knew me, have forgotten the very name of Toad!

"Oh, wise old Badger! Oh, clever, intelligent Rat and sensible Mole! What sound judgments, what a knowledge of men and matters you possess! Oh, unhappy and forsaken Toad!" With lamentations such as these he passed his days and nights for several weeks.

Now the jailer had a daughter who assisted

her father in the lighter duties of his post. She was particularly fond of animals, and, pitying the misery of Toad, knocked one day at the door of his cell.

"Now, cheer up, Toad," she said coaxingly, on entering, "and sit up and dry your eyes and be a sensible animal." She carried a tray with a cup of fragrant tea steaming on it, and a plate with very hot buttered toast. The smell of that buttered toast simply talked to Toad— talked of warm kitchens, of breakfast on bright frosty mornings, of cozy parlor firesides on winter evenings, of the purring of contented cats, and the twitter of sleepy canaries. Toad sat up, dried his eyes, sipped his tea and munched his toast, and soon began talking freely about himself, and the house he lived in.

The jailer's daughter encouraged him to go on. "Tell me about Toad Hall," she said. "It sounds beautiful."

"Toad Hall," said the Toad proudly, "is a self-contained gentleman's residence, very unique, dating in part from the fourteenth century, but having every modern convenience. Up-to-date sanitation. Five minutes from church, post office, and golf links."

Continuing, his spirits quite restored to their usual level, Toad told her about the boathouse, and the fishpond, and the old walled kitchen garden; and about the pigsties, and the stables, and the henhouse; and about the dairy, and the washhouse, and the china cupboards, and the banqueting hall, and the fun they had there when the other animals were gathered round the table.

Then she wanted to know about his animal friends, and was very interested in all he had to tell her about them and how they lived. When she said good night, the Toad was very much the same self-satisfied animal that he had been of old. He sang a little song or two, and then had an excellent night's rest and the pleasantest of dreams.

They had many interesting talks together after that. The jailer's daughter thought it a great shame that a poor little animal should be locked up in prison for what seemed to her a very trivial offense.

One morning the girl was very thoughtful.

"Toad," she said presently, "just listen, please. I have an aunt who is a washerwoman. She does the washing for all the prisoners in this castle.

"Now, this is what occurs to me: you're very rich—at least you're always telling me so—and she's very poor. A few pounds wouldn't make any difference to you, and it would mean a lot to her. I think you could come to some arrangement by which she would let you have her dress and bonnet and so on, and you could escape from the castle as the official washerwoman."

"You are a good, kind, clever girl," said Toad. "Introduce me to your worthy aunt, if you will be so kind, and I have no doubt that the excellent lady and I will be able to arrange terms."

Next evening the girl ushered her aunt into Toad's cell, bearing his week's washing pinned up in a towel. In return for his cash, Toad received a cotton print gown, an apron, a shawl, and a rusty black bonnet. "Now, Toad," said the girl, "take off that coat and waistcoat of yours. You're fat enough as it is."

Shaking with laughter, she proceeded to

"hook-and-eye" him into the cotton print gown, arranged the shawl, and tied the strings of the rusty bonnet under his chin.

"You're the very image of her," she giggled, "only I'm sure you never looked half so respectable in all your life before. Now, good-bye, Toad, and good luck. Go straight down the way you came up."

With a quaking heart, Toad set forth cautiously on what seemed to be a most harebrained and hazardous undertaking. But he was soon agreeably surprised to find how easy everything was. The washerwoman's squat figure in its familiar cotton print seemed a passport for every barred door and gateway.

At last he heard the wicket gate in the great outer door click behind him, felt the fresh air of the outer world upon his anxious brow, and knew that he was free!

He made his way to the railroad station, consulted a timetable, and found that a train, bound more or less in the direction of his home, was due to start in half an hour. "What luck!" said Toad, his spirits rising rapidly, and went to buy his ticket.

But when he put his fingers, in search of

the necessary money, where his waistcoat pocket should have been, he found—not only no money, but no pocket to hold it, and no waistcoat to hold the pocket! To his horror he recollected that he had left both coat and waistcoat behind him in his cell. In his misery he made one desperate effort to carry the thing off, and said, "Look here! I find I've left my purse behind. Just give me that ticket, will you, and I'll send the money on tomorrow. I'm known in these parts."

The clerk stared at him and then laughed. "I should think you were pretty well known in these parts," he said, "if you've tried this game often. Stand away from the window, please, madam."

Baffled and full of despair, he wandered blindly down the platform where the train was standing, and tears trickled down each side of his nose.

"Hullo, mother!" said the engine driver. "What's the trouble?"

"Oh, sir!" said Toad, crying afresh, "I am a poor unhappy washerwoman, and I've lost all my money, and can't pay for a ticket, and I *must* get home tonight somehow, and whatever I am to do I don't know. Oh, dear! Oh, dear!"

"Well, I'll tell you what I'll do," said the good engine driver. "If you wash a few shirts for me when you get home, and send 'em along, I'll give you a ride on my engine. It's against regulations, but we're not so very particular in these out-of-the-way parts."

The Toad's misery turned into rapture as he eagerly scrambled up into the cab of the engine. Of course, he had never washed a shirt in his life, and couldn't if he tried, but he thought, "When I get safely home to Toad Hall, and have money again, I will send the engine driver enough to pay for a washing, and that will be the same thing, or better."

The train moved out of the station, and as the speed increased, the Toad could see on either side of him real fields and trees, and hedges, and cows, and horses. As he thought how every minute was bringing him nearer to Toad Hall, and sympathetic friends, and money to chink in his pocket, and a soft bed to sleep in, and good things to eat, he began to skip and shout and sing snatches of song, to the great astonishment of the engine driver.

They had covered many and many a mile when Toad noticed that the engine driver, with a puzzled expression on his face, was leaning over the side of the engine and listening hard. Then he saw him climb on to the coals and gaze out over the top of the train. He returned and said to Toad, "It's very strange. We're the last train running in this direction tonight, yet it looks as if were being pursued!"

The miserable Toad, crouching in the coal dust, tried hard to think of something to do, with dismal want of success.

"They are gaining on us fast!" cried the engine driver. "And the engine is crowded with policemen and plainclothes detectives, waving revolvers and sticks, all waving, and shouting the same thing—'Stop, stop, stop!'"

Then Toad fell on his knees among the coals and, raising his clasped paws, cried, "Save me, dear, kind Mr. Engine driver, and I will confess everything! I am not the simple washerwoman I seem to be! I am a toad—the well-known and popular Mr. Toad. I have just escaped, by daring and cleverness, from a dungeon, and if those fellows on that engine recapture me, it will be chains and bread and water and straw and *misery* once more for poor, unhappy, innocent Toad!"

The engine driver looked very grave and said, "I fear that you have been indeed a wicked toad, and by rights I ought to give you up to justice. But the sight of an animal in tears always makes me soft-hearted. So cheer up, Toad! I'll do my best, and we may beat them yet!"

They piled on more coals, shoveling furiously, and the train shot into a tunnel, and the engine rushed and roared and rattled, till at last they shot out at the other end into fresh air and saw a wood upon either side of the line. The driver shut off steam and put on brakes. Toad jumped, rolled down a short embankment, picked himself up unhurt, scrambled into the wood and hid.

Peeping out, he saw his train get up speed again and disappear. Then out of the tunnel burst the pursuing engine, roaring and whistling, her motley crew waving their weapons and shouting, "Stop! stop! stop!" When they were past, the Toad had a hearty laugh—for the first time since he was thrown into prison.

But he soon stopped laughing when he came to consider that it was now very late and dark and cold, and he was in an unknown wood, with no money and no chance of supper, and still far from friends and home. He dared not leave the shelter of the trees, so he struck into the wood and sought the safety of a hollow tree, where with branches and dead leaves he made himself as comfortable a bed as he could, and slept soundly till morning.

7

The Further Adventures of Toad

The front door of the hollow tree faced eastward, so Toad was roused at an early hour, partly by the bright sunlight streaming in on him, partly by the coldness of his toes. Sitting up, he rubbed his eyes first and his complaining toes next, wondering where he was. He shook himself and combed the dry leaves out of his hair with his fingers. He marched forth into the comfortable morning sun, cold but confident, hungry but hopeful.

Toad had the world all to himself that early summer morning. The dewy woodland was solitary and still. The road, when he reached it, in the center of the surrounding loneliness, seemed like a stray dog, anxious for company. Toad, however, was looking for someone who could speak and explain which way he ought to go.

It is all very well to follow where the road leads, not caring which direction. But Toad cared very much, and he could have kicked the road for its silence when every minute was of importance to him.

The road was presently joined by a canal, which ran alongside.

"One thing's clear," Toad said to himself. "They must both be coming *from* somewhere, and going *to* somewhere." So he marched on patiently by the water's edge.

Round a bend in the canal came a solitary horse, stooping forward as if in anxious thought. From rope traces attached to his collar stretched a long line. Toad stood waiting as the horse passed.

With a swirl of water at its bow a barge slid up alongside him. Its sole occupant was a big stout woman wearing a linen sunbonnet. One of her brawny arms rested upon the tiller.

"A nice morning, ma'am!" she remarked to Toad as she drew up level with him.

"I dare say it is, ma'am!" responded Toad politely as he walked along the towpath aside her. "I dare say it is a nice morning to them that's not in sore trouble, like what I am. Here's my married daughter, she sends a message for me to come to her at once. So off I comes, not knowing what may be happening or going to happen, but fearing the worst, as you will understand, ma'am, if you're a mother. And I've left my young children to look after themselves, and a more mischievous and troublesome set of young imps doesn't exist, and I've lost my money and lost my way."

"Where might your married daughter be living, ma'am?" asked the bargewoman.

"She lives near to the river, ma'am," replied Toad. "Close to a fine house called Toad Hall. Perhaps you may have heard of it."

"Toad Hall? Why, I'm going that way myself," replied the bargewoman. "Come along in the barge with me, and I'll give you a lift."

She steered the barge close to the bank, and Toad, with many thanks, stepped lightly on board and sat down with great satisfaction. "Toad's luck again!" thought he. "I always come out on top."

"You're in the washing business, ma'am?"

said the bargewoman politely as they glided along.

"Finest business in the whole country," said Toad. "The best customers come to me. You see, I understand my work thoroughly and attend to it all myself. Washing, ironing, starching, making up gents' fine shirts for evening wear—everything's done under my own eye!"

"And you are very fond of washing?" asked the bargewoman.

"I love it," said Toad. "I'm never so happy as when I've got both arms in the washtub. But, then, it comes so easy to me! No trouble at all!"

"What a bit of luck, meeting you!" observed the bargewoman thoughtfully. "A regular piece of good fortune for both of us!"

"Why, what do you mean?" asked Toad nervously.

"Well, look at me, now," replied the bargewoman. "*I* like washing, too, just the same as you do. And, naturally, moving about as I do, I have to do all my own. Now my husband, he's such a fellow for avoiding work and leaving the barge to me, that never a moment do I get for seeing to my own affairs. And how am I to get on with my washing?"

"Oh, never mind about the washing," said Toad, not liking the subject. "Try and fix your mind on that rabbit. Got any onions?"

"I can't fix my mind on anything but my washing," said the bargewoman, "and I wonder you can be talking of rabbits, with such a joyful prospect before you. There's a heap of things of mine that you'll find in a corner of the cabin. There's also a tub, and soap, and a kettle on the stove, and a bucket to haul up water from the canal with. Then I shall know you're enjoying yourself, instead of sitting here idle."

"Here, you let me steer!" said Toad, now thoroughly frightened, "and then you can get on with your washing your own way."

"Let you steer?" replied the bargewoman, laughing. "It takes some practice to steer a barge properly. No, you shall do the washing you are so fond of, and I'll stick to steering."

The Toad was fairly cornered. He looked for escape, but saw that he was too far from the bank for a flying leap. "If it comes to that," he thought in desperation, "I suppose any fool can *wash!*"

He fetched a tub, soap, and other items from the cabin, selected a few garments, and tried to remember what he had seen in glancing through laundry windows. A half hour passed, and every minute of it saw Toad getting crosser and crosser. Nothing he did to clean the laundry seemed to work. His back ached badly, and he noticed with dismay that his paws were getting all crinkly. He muttered under his breath, and lost the soap for the fiftieth time.

A burst of laughter made him straighten up and look around. The bargewoman was leaning back and laughing till tears ran down her cheeks.

"I've been watching you all the time," she gasped. "Pretty washerwoman you are! Never washed so much as a dish cloth in your life, I'll bet!"

Toad's temper boiled over, and he lost all control of himself. "You common, *fat* bargewoman!" he shouted. "I would have you know that I am a very well-known, respected, distinguished Toad!"

The woman moved nearer to him and peered under his bonnet. "Why, so you are!" she cried. "A horrid, nasty, crawly Toad! And in my nice clean barge, too!"

She left the tiller and caught Toad by a fore-leg, while her other hand gripped a hind leg. The world turned suddenly upside down, the wind whistled in Toad's ears, and he found himself flying through the air, revolving rapidly as he went. He reached the water with a loud splash, but its chill was not enough to quell his proud spirit or cool his furious temper. As he coughed and spluttered, he saw the bargewoman looking back at him over the stern of the retreating barge and laughing.

Toad vowed to get even with her. He scrambled up the steep bank with difficulty and had to rest a few minutes to recover his breath. Then, gathering his wet skirts well over his arms, he started to run after the barge as fast as his legs would carry him, wild with indignation, thirsting for revenge.

The bargewoman was still laughing when he drew up level with her. "Soak and iron your face," she called out, "and you'll pass for quite a decent-looking Toad!"

Toad never paused to reply. Running swiftly, he overtook the horse, unfastened the towrope and cast off. Then he hopped on the horse's back and urged it to a gallop by kicking it vigorously in the sides. Heading for open country, he looked back and saw that the barge had run aground on the other side of the canal. The bargewoman was gesturing wildly and shouting, "Stop, stop, stop!"

The barge horse was not capable of any sustained effort, and its gallop soon slowed to a trot, then to an easy walk. But Toad was quite content with this, knowing that he, at any rate, was moving, and the barge was not. He tried to forget how very long it was since he had had a decent meal.

He had traveled some miles, and he was feeling drowsy in the hot sunshine. When the horse stopped, lowered his head, and began to nibble the grass, Toad woke up and just saved himself from falling off by an effort.

He looked about and saw a dingy gypsy caravan. Beside it a man was sitting on an up-turned bucket, busy smoking and staring straight ahead. A fire was burning nearby, and over the fire hung an iron pot that

Susan Wheeler

steamed and bubbled and gurgled. It gave off a wonderful smell.

The Toad realized that he had never been so hungry. He looked the gypsy over carefully, wondering whether it would be easier to fight him or coax him for some food. So there he sat, and sniffed and sniffed, and looked at the gypsy. And the gypsy sat and smoked, and stared at him.

Presently the gypsy took his pipe out of his mouth and asked in a casual manner, "Want to sell that there horse of yours?"

Toad was taken completely by surprise. He did not know that gypsies were very fond of horse-trading. It had not occurred to him to turn the horse into cash. However, he needed two things badly: ready money and a solid breakfast.

"What?" he said. "Me sell this beautiful young horse of mine? Oh, no. It's out of the question. Who's going to take the washing home to my customers every week? Besides, I'm too fond of him, and he adores me."

"Try and love a donkey," suggested the gypsy.

"You don't seem to realize," Toad continued, "that this fine horse of mine comes from prize stock. No, I couldn't consider selling her. All the same, how much might you be disposed to offer for this beautiful young horse of mine?"

The gypsy looked the horse over, and then he looked Toad over with equal care, and examined the horse again. "A shilling a leg," he said briefly, and turned away.

"A shilling a leg?" Toad cried. "I must take a little time to work that out and see just what it amounts to."

He climbed down off his horse and sat down by the gypsy. Doing addition on his fingers, he finally said, "A shilling a leg? Why, that comes to exactly four shillings, and no more. Oh, no. I could not think of accepting four shillings for this beautiful young horse of mine."

"Well," said the gypsy, "I'll make it five shillings, and that's more than the animal's worth. That's my last word."

Toad sat pondering long and deeply. On the one hand, he was hungry and quite penniless, and still some way from home, with enemies possibly looking for him. On the other hand, it did not seem very much to get for a horse. But then again, the horse hadn't cost him anything. At last he said firmly, "Look here, gypsy! This is *my* last word. Hand me over six shillings and sixpence, cash down, in addition to as much breakfast as I can possibly eat at one sitting, out of that iron pot of yours. In return, I will give you my spirited young horse and throw in its beautiful harness and trappings."

The gypsy grumbled, but in the end he lugged a dirty canvas bag out of his pocket and counted out six shillings and sixpence into Toad's paw. Then he disappeared into the caravan for an instant, returning with a large iron plate and a knife, fork, and spoon. He tilted the pot, and a glorious stream of hot rich stew gurgled into the plate. Almost crying, Toad took the plate on his lap, and stuffed and stuffed, and kept asking for more. The gypsy never refused.

When Toad had eaten as much stew as his stomach could possibly hold, he got up and said good-bye to the gypsy. He gave the horse an affectionate pat, and the gypsy pointed out the direction to go. So Toad set forth on his travels again, in high spirits. The sun was shining brightly, his wet clothes were dry again, he had money in his pocket once more, and he was nearing home and friends and safety.

As he tramped along, he thought of his adventures and escapes, and how when things seemed at their worst he had always managed to find a way out. "Ho, ho!" he said to himself as he marched along with his chin in the air. "What a clever Toad I am! There is surely no animal equal to me for cleverness in the whole world!"

After some miles of country lanes he reached the highroad. As he turned into it and glanced along its length, he saw approaching him a speck that turned into a dot, and then into a blob, and then into something very familiar.

He stepped confidently out into the road to hail the motorcar, which came along at an easy pace, slowing down as it neared the lane. Suddenly he became very pale, his heart turned to water, and his knees shook and yielded under him. The approaching car was the very one he had stolen out of the yard of the Red Lion Hotel on that fatal day when all his troubles began!

He sank down in a shabby, miserable heap in the road, murmuring to himself in his despair, "It's all up! It's all over now! Chains and policemen again! Prison again! Dry bread and water again!"

The terrible motorcar drew slowly nearer and nearer, till at last he heard it stop just short of him. Two gentlemen got out and walked round the trembling heap lying in the road, and one of them said, "Oh, dear! This is very sad! Here is a poor old thing—a washerwoman apparently—who has fainted in the road! Let us lift her into the car and take her to the nearest village, where doubtless she has friends."

They tenderly lifted Toad into the motorcar and propped him up with soft cushions, and proceeded on their way.

When Toad heard them talk in so kind and sympathetic a manner, and knew that he was not recognized, his courage began to revive, and he cautiously opened first one eye and then the other.

"Look!" said one of the gentlemen, "she is

better already. The fresh air is doing her good. How do you feel now, ma'am?"

"Thank you kindly, sir," said Toad in a feeble voice, "I'm feeling a great deal better!"

Toad was almost himself again by now. He sat up, looked about him, and turned to the driver at his side.

"Please, sir," he said, "I wish you would kindly let me try and drive the car for a little. I've been watching you carefully, and it looks so easy and so interesting, and I should like to be able to tell my friends that once I had driven a motorcar!"

The driver laughed good-naturedly at the proposal, and said, to Toad's delight, "Bravo, ma'am! I like your spirit. Have a try!" Toad eagerly scrambled into the seat vacated by the driver, took the steering wheel in his hands, and set the car in motion—very slowly and carefully at first.

Toad went a little faster, then faster still, and faster. He put on full speed. The rush of air on his face, the hum of the engine, and the light jump of the car beneath him intoxicated his brain.

"Washerwoman, indeed!" he shouted recklessly. "Ho! ho! I am the Toad, the motorcar snatcher, the prison breaker—the Toad who always escapes! Sit still, and you shall know what driving really is. You are in the hands of the famous, the skillful, the entirely fearless Toad!"

With a cry of horror the whole party rose and flung themselves on him. "Seize him!" they cried. "Seize the Toad, the wicked animal who stole our motorcar! Bind him, chain him, drag him to the nearest police station! Down with the desperate and dangerous Toad!"

Alas! They should have thought. They should have remembered to stop the motorcar somehow before playing any pranks of that sort. With a half-turn of the wheel, the Toad sent the car crashing through the low hedge that ran along the roadside. One mighty bound, a violent shock, and the wheels of the car were churning up the thick mud of a horsepond.

Toad found himself flying through the air and was just beginning to wonder whether it would go on until he developed wings and turned into a Toad-bird, when he landed on his back in the soft rich grass of a meadow.

He picked himself up rapidly, and set off running across country as hard as he could, scrambling through hedges, jumping ditches, pounding across fields, till he was breathless and weary. Suddenly the earth failed under his feet. He grasped at the air and found himself head over ears in deep water, rapid water, water that bore him along. He had run straight into the river!

He rose to the surface and tried to grasp the reeds and the rushes that grew along the water's edge close under the bank, but the stream was so strong that it tore them out of his hands. Presently he saw that he was approaching a big dark hole in the bank, just above his head, and as the stream bore him past, he reached up with a paw and caught hold of the edge and held on.

As he stared before him into the dark hole, some bright, small thing shone and twinkled in its depths, moving toward him. A face grew up gradually around it, and it was a familiar face! Brown and small with whiskers. Grave and round, with neat ears and silky hair. It was the Water Rat!

8

Reunion of Friends

The Rat put out a neat little brown paw, gripped Toad firmly by the scruff of the neck, and gave a great hoist and a pull. The waterlogged Toad came up slowly over the edge of the hole. At last he stood safe and sound in the hall, the water streaming off him. He was happy to find himself once more in the house of a friend.

"Oh, Ratty!" he cried. "I've been through such times since I saw you last, you can't think! Such trials, such sufferings, and all so nobly borne! Then such escapes, such disguises, such ruses, and all so cleverly planned and carried out! Been in prison—got out of it, of course! Humbugged everybody—made 'em all do exactly what I wanted! Oh, I *am* a smart Toad, and no mistake!"

"Toad," said the Water Rat gravely and firmly, "you go off upstairs at once, and take off that old cotton rag that looks as if it might formerly have belonged to some washerwoman, and clean yourself thoroughly, and put on some of my clothes and try and come down looking like a gentleman if you can. A more shabby, bedraggled, disreputable-looking object than you are I never set eyes on in my whole life! Now, stop swaggering and arguing, and be off! I'll have something to say to you later!"

By the time Toad came down again, luncheon was on the table. While they ate, he told the Rat all his adventures, dwelling chiefly on his own cleverness, and presence of mind in emergencies.

When at last Toad had finished his tale, he said, "Now I'm going to stroll gently down to Toad Hall, and get into clothes of my own, and set things going again on the old lines. I've had enough of adventures. From now on, I shall lead a quiet, steady, respectable life."

"Stroll gently down to Toad Hall?" cried

the Rat, greatly excited. "Do you mean to say you haven't *heard*?"

"Heard what?" said Toad, turning rather pale. "Go on, Ratty! Don't spare me! What haven't I heard?"

"Do you mean to tell me," shouted the Rat, thumping the table with his little fist, "that you've heard nothing about the Stoats and Weasels and how they've taken Toad Hall?"

"What, the Wild Wooders?" cried Toad. He leaned his elbows on the table and his chin on his paws. A large tear welled up in each of his eyes and splashed on the table, *plop! plop!*

"Go on, Ratty," he murmured presently, "tell me all. The worst is over. I can bear it."

"When you—got—into that—that—trouble of yours," said the Rat slowly and haltingly, "I mean, when you—disappeared for a time, over that misunderstanding about a—a machine, you know—"

Toad merely nodded.

"Well, it was a good deal talked about down here, naturally," continued the Rat, "not only along the riverside, but even in the Wild Wood. The River-bankers stuck up for you, and said you had been unfairly treated, and there was no justice. But the Wild Wood animals said harsh things. They said it served you right, and you would never come back again, never!"

Toad nodded once more, keeping silence.

"Mole and Badger insisted you would come back again soon, somehow," the Rat went on. "So they arranged to move their things into Toad Hall, and sleep there, and keep it aired, and have it all ready for you when you turned up. They had their suspicions of the Wild Wood animals.

"One dark, rainy night, a band of weasels—armed to the teeth—crept silently up the carriage drive to the front entrance. At the same time, a body of ferrets, advancing through the kitchen garden, took over the backyard and offices. And a company of stoats occupied the conservatory and the billiard room.

"Mole and Badger were sitting by the fire in the smoking room, telling stories and suspecting nothing, when those bloodthirsty villains broke down the doors and rushed in upon them from every side. They made the best fight they could, but what was the good? They were unarmed, and taken by surprise. What can two animals do against hundreds? The Wild Wooders beat them severely with sticks and turned them out into the cold and the wet, with many insulting remarks!"

Here the unfeeling Toad broke into a snigger, and then pulled himself together and tried to look particularly solemn.

"And the Wild Wooders have been living in Toad Hall ever since," continued the Rat. "The place is such a mess, I'm told. They're eating your food, and drinking your drink, and making bad jokes about you. And they're telling everybody that they've come to stay for good."

"Oh, have they!" said Toad, getting up and seizing a stick. "I'll soon see about that!"

"It's no good, Toad!" called the Rat after him. "You'd better come back and sit down. You'll only get into trouble."

But the Toad went off, and there was no holding him.

When he reached his front gate, he met a long, yellow ferret with a gun. "Who comes there?" said the ferret sharply.

"Stuff and nonsense!" said Toad angrily.

The ferret brought his gun up to his shoulder, and *Bang!* a bullet whistled over Toad's head. He scampered off down the road as fast as he could; and as he ran, he heard the ferret laughing. Other ferrets immediately joined in.

"What did I tell you?" said the Rat when Toad returned. "It's no good. They've got sentries posted, and they are all armed. You must just wait."

But Toad got out the boat and set off rowing up the river. Very warily he paddled within sight of his old home, and was just passing under the bridge, when . . . *crash!* A great stone, dropped from above, smashed through the bottom of the boat. It filled and sank, and Toad found himself struggling in deep water. The indignant Toad swam to shore, while two stoats on the bridge above laughed and laughed.

The Toad retraced his weary way on foot, and related his disappointing experiences to the Water Rat once more.

"Well, *what* did I tell you?" said the Rat very crossly.

The Toad made a full apology to Rat for losing his boat and spoiling his clothes. "Ratty!

Henceforth, believe me, I will take no action without your kind advice and full approval!"

"If that is really so," said the good-natured Rat, "then my advice to you is to sit down and have your supper, which will be on the table in a minute."

"What's become of Mole and Badger, the dear fellows?" Toad asked.

"While you have been riding about the country, they have been keeping a constant eye on the stoats and the weasels, scheming and planning how to get your property back for you."

"I'm an ungrateful beast, I know," Toad sobbed.

After they had finished their meal, a heavy knock came at the door. Rat opened it, and in walked Mr. Badger. He had the appearance of one who had been kept away from home for nights.

He shook Toad's paw and said, "Welcome home, Toad! Alas! what am I saying? Home, indeed! This is a poor homecoming." Then he drew a chair up to the table and helped himself to a large slice of cold pie.

Presently Mole arrived, very shabby and

unwashed. "Hooray! Here's old Toad!" he cried, his face beaming. And he began to dance around him. "We never dreamed you would turn up so soon. Why, you must have managed to escape, you clever, ingenious, intelligent Toad!"

The Rat pulled him by the elbow, but it was too late. Toad was puffing and swelling with pride. "Clever? Oh, no!" he said. "I'm not really clever, according to my friends. I've only broken out of the strongest prison in England, that's all! And captured a railway train and escaped on it, that's all! And disguised myself and gone about the country fooling everybody, that's all! Oh, no! I'm stupid, I am!"

"Well, well," said the Mole, moving toward the supper table, "suppose you tell me your adventures while I eat." He sat down and helped himself to cold beef and pickles.

The Toad thrust his paw into his trouser pocket and pulled out a handful of coins. "Look at that!" he cried, displaying them. "That's not so bad, is it, for a few minutes' work? And how do you think I done it, Mole? Horse dealing! That's how I done it!"

"Go on, Toad," said the Mole, immensely interested.

"Toad, do be quiet, please!" said the Rat. "And don't you egg him on, Mole. But please tell us what the position is, and what's to be done, now that Toad is back at last."

"The position's about as bad as it can be," replied the Mole, "and as for what's to be done, why, blest if I know! The Badger and I have been round and round the place, by night and by day. Sentries are posted everywhere. Guns poked out at us, stones were thrown. And when they see us, my! How they do laugh! That's what annoys me most!"

When the Badger had finished eating, he got up from his seat and stood before the fireplace, thinking deeply. At last he spoke. "Toad!" he said severely. "You bad, troublesome little animal! What do you think your father, my old friend, would have said if he had been here tonight, and had known of all your goings on?"

Toad, who was on the sofa by this time, rolled over on his face, shaken by sobs of remorse.

"There, there!" went on the Badger more

kindly. "Never mind. Stop crying. We're going to try to turn over a new leaf. But what Mole says is quite true. The stoats are on guard at every point, and they make the best sentries in the world. It's quite useless to think of attacking the place. They're too strong for us."

"Then it's all over," sobbed the Toad. "I shall never see my dear Toad Hall anymore!"

"Come, cheer up, Toady!" said Badger. "There are more ways of getting back a place than taking it by storm. Now I'm going to tell you a great secret. There is an underground passage that leads from the river bank, quite near here, right up into the middle of Toad Hall."

"Oh, nonsense, Badger!" said Toad. "I know every inch of Toad Hall, inside and out. Nothing of the sort, I do assure you!"

"My young friend," said the Badger severely, "your father was a close friend of mine. He discovered that passage, and he repaired it and cleaned it out. 'Don't let my son know about it,' he said. 'He's a good boy, but simply cannot hold his tongue. If he's ever in real trouble or danger, and it would be of use to him, you may tell him about the secret passage. But not before.'"

"Well, well," Toad said after pouting a bit, "perhaps I am a bit of a talker. I have the gift of conversation. Never mind. Go on, Badger. How's this passage of yours going to help us?"

"I've found out a thing or two lately," continued the Badger. "I got Otter to disguise himself as a chimney sweep and call at the back door, asking for a job. There's going to be a big banquet tomorrow night. It's the Chief Weasel's birthday, I believe, and all the weasels will be gathered together in the dining hall, eating and drinking and laughing and carrying on, suspecting nothing. No guns, no swords, no sticks, no arms of any sort whatever!"

"But the sentries will be posted as usual," remarked the Rat.

"Exactly," said Badger. "The weasels will put their trust entirely in their excellent sentries. And that is where the passage comes in. That very useful tunnel leads right up under the butler's pantry, next to the dining hall!"

"Aha! That squeaky board in the butler's

pantry!" said Toad. "Now I understand it!"

"We shall creep out quietly into the butler's pantry—"cried the Mole.

"—with our pistols and swords and sticks—" shouted the Rat.

"—and rush in upon them," said the Badger.

"—and whack 'em, and whack 'em, and whack 'em!" cried the Toad in ecstasy, running round and round the room.

"Very well, then," said the Badger, resuming his usual dry manner, "our plan is settled. As it's getting very late, all of you go right off to bed at once. We will make all the necessary arrangements tomorrow morning."

Toad went off to bed dutifully with the others—he knew better than to refuse—though he was feeling much too excited to sleep. But he had had a long day, with many events crowded into it, and sheets and blankets felt very comfortable after the straw of his prison cell. His head had not been many seconds on the pillow before he was snoring happily.

He slept till a late hour next morning, and by the time he got downstairs he found that the other animals had finished their breakfast some time before. The Mole had slipped off somewhere by himself, without telling anyone where he was going. The Badger sat in the armchair, reading the paper, quite unconcerned about what was going to happen that very evening.

The Rat, on the other hand, was running round the room busily, with his arms full of weapons of every kind, distributing them in four little heaps on the floor.

"That's all very well, Rat," said the Badger, looking at the busy little animal over the edge of his newspaper. "But just let us once get past the stoats, with those guns of theirs, and I assure you we won't need any swords or pistols. Once we're inside the dining hall, we four, with our sticks, will mop up the floor with them in five minutes."

"It's as well to be on the safe side," said the Rat, polishing a pistol-barrel on his sleeve.

The Toad, having finished his breakfast, picked up a stick and swung it vigorously. "I'll learn 'em to steal my house!"

"Don't say 'learn 'em,' Toad," said the Rat, greatly shocked. "It's not good English."

"What's the matter with Toad's English?"

Badger inquired peevishly. "It's the same what I use myself."

"I'm very sorry," said the Rat humbly. "Only I *think* it ought to be 'teach 'em,' not 'learn 'em.' But have it your own way."

Presently the Mole came running into the room, evidently pleased with himself. "I've been having such fun at the stoats' expense!"

"I hope you've been very careful, Mole!" said the Rat anxiously.

"I should hope so, too," said the Mole confidently. "I got the idea when I found that old washerwoman dress that Toad came home in yesterday. I put it on, and the bonnet as well, and the shawl, and off I went to Toad Hall, as bold as you please. 'Good morning, gentlemen!' says I to the sentries. 'Want any washing done today?'

"They looked at me very proud and stiff and haughty, and said, 'Go away, washerwoman! We don't do any washing on duty.' 'Or any other time?' says I. Ho, ho, ho. Wasn't I *funny*, Toad?"

It was exactly what Toad would have liked to have done himself, if only he had thought of it first. He felt jealous.

"Some of the stoats turned quite pink," continued the Mole, "and the sergeant in charge, he said to me, 'Now run away, my good woman!' 'Run away?' says I. 'It won't be me that'll be running away, in a very short time from now!'"

"Oh, *Moly*, how could you?" said the Rat, dismayed.

"I could see them pricking up their ears and looking at each other," the Mole went on. "The sergeant said to them, 'Never mind her. She doesn't know what she's talking about.'

"'My daughter, she washes for Mr. Badger,' said I, 'and that'll show you whether I know what I'm talking about. And *you'll* know pretty soon, too! A hundred blood-thirsty Badgers, armed with rifles, are going to attack Toad Hall this very night, by way of the paddock. Six boatloads of Rats, with pistols and swords, will come up the river, while a picked body of Toads will storm the orchard, yelling for vengeance. There won't be much left of you to wash, by the time they're done with you, unless you clear out while you have the chance!'

"Then I ran away and hid and took a peep

at them through the hedge. They were all as nervous as could be, running all ways at once, and falling over each other. The sergeant kept sending out parties of stoats to distant parts of the grounds. And I heard them saying to each other, 'That's *just* like the weasels. They're going to feast in the banquet hall, with toasts and songs and all sorts of fun, while we must stay on guard in the cold and the dark, and in the end be cut to pieces by bloodthirsty Badgers!'"

"Oh, you foolish Mole!" cried the Toad. "You've gone and spoiled everything!"

"Mole," said the Badger, "I see you have more sense in your little finger than some other animals have in the whole of their fat bodies. Good Mole! Clever Mole!"

The Toad was simply wild with jealousy, more especially as he couldn't figure out what the Mole had done that was so particularly clever.

The bell rang for luncheon. It was a simple but substantial meal—bacon and broad beans, and a macaroni pudding. When they were done, the Badger settled himself into an armchair and said, "We've got our work cut out for us tonight, and it will probably be pretty late before we're quite through with it. So I'm just going to take forty winks while I can." And he drew a handkerchief over his face and was soon snoring.

The anxious and busy Rat at once resumed his preparations, and started running between his four little heaps muttering, "Here's-a-sword-for-the-Rat, here's-a-sword-for-the-Mole, here's-a-sword-for-the-Toad, here's-a-sword-for-the-Badger!" and so on with every new weapon he produced, to which there seemed no end.

The Mole drew his arm through the Toad's, led him out into the open air, shoved him into a wicker chair, and made him tell all his adventures from beginning to end, which the Toad was only too willing to do. The Mole was a good listener, and the Toad let himself go in relating his raciest adventures. However, much of what he related did not actually happen but was in the category of what-might-have-happened-had-I-only-thought-of-it-in-time-instead-of-ten-minutes-afterwards.

9

The Return of Toad

When it began to grow dark, the Rat, with an air of excitement and mystery, called them back into the parlor, lined each of them up alongside his little heap, and proceeded to dress them for the coming adventure. He was very earnest and thorough, and the affair took quite a long time. First, there was a belt to go around each animal, and then a sword to be stuck into each belt, and then a cutlass on the other side. Then a pair of pistols, a policeman's club, several sets of handcuffs, some bandages, and adhesive tape.

The Badger laughed good-humoredly and said, "All right, Ratty! It amuses you, and it doesn't hurt me. I'm going to do all I've got to do with this here stick."

When all was quite ready, the Badger took a dark lantern in one paw, grasped his great stick with the other, and said, "Now then, follow me! Mole first, 'cause I'm very pleased with him; Rat next; Toad last. And look here, Toady! Don't you chatter so much as usual, or you'll be sent back!"

The Toad was so anxious not to be left out that he took up the position assigned to him without a murmur, and the animals set off. The Badger led them along by the river for a little way, and then suddenly swung himself over the edge into a hole in the river bank, a little above the water. The Mole and the Rat followed silently, swinging themselves successfully into the hole as they had seen the Badger do.

But when it came to Toad's turn, of course he managed to slip and fall into the water with a loud splash and a squeal of alarm. He was hauled out by his friends, rubbed down and wrung out hastily, comforted, and set on his legs. But the Badger was seriously angry, and told him that the very next time he made a fool of himself he would most certainly be left behind.

At last they were in the secret passage. It was cold and dark, and damp, and low, and narrow. Poor Toad began to shiver, partly from dread of what might be before him, partly because he was wet through. The lantern was far ahead, and he could not help trailing behind a little in the darkness. Then he heard the Rat call out warningly, "*Come* on, Toad!" and a terror seized him of being left behind, alone in the darkness. So he lunged forward with such a rush that he shoved the Rat into the Mole, and the Mole into the Badger, and for a moment all was confusion.

The Badger thought they were being attacked from behind, and, as there was no room to use a stick, drew a pistol and was about to put a bullet into Toad. When he found out what had really happened he was very angry indeed, and said, "Now this time that tiresome Toad *shall* be left behind!"

But Toad whimpered, and the other two promised to answer for his good conduct, and at last the Badger was satisfied, and the procession moved on. Only this time the Rat brought up the rear, with a firm grip on the shoulder of Toad.

So they groped along, with their ears pricked up and their paws on their pistols, till at last the Badger said, "We ought by now to be pretty nearly under the Hall."

Then suddenly they heard, muffled yet apparently over their heads, a confused murmur of sound, as if people were shouting and cheering and stamping on the floor and thumping tables. The Toad's nervous fears all returned, but the Badger only remarked calmly. "The weasels are having a time of it!"

The passage now began to slope upward. They groped on a little farther, and the noise broke out again, more distinctly this time and very close above them. "Hoo-ray—hoo-ray—hoo-ray!" they heard, and the stamping of little feet pounded on the table.

They hurried along the passage till it came to a full stop, and they found themselves standing under the trapdoor that led up into the butler's pantry.

Such a tremendous noise was going on in the banquet hall that there was little danger of their being overheard. The Badger said, "Now, boys, all together!" and the four of them put their shoulders to the trapdoor and heaved it back. Hoisting each other up, they found themselves standing in the pantry, with only a door between them and the banquet hall, where their enemies were carrying on. The noise was deafening.

As the cheering and hammering slowly subsided, they made out a voice saying, "I should like to say one word about our kind host, Mr. Toad. We all know Toad!"—great laughter—"*Good* Toad, *modest* Toad, *honest* Toad!" This was followed by shrieks of merriment.

"Only just let me get at him!" muttered Toad, grinding his teeth.

"Hold hard a minute!" said the Badger, restraining him with difficulty. "Get ready, all of you!"

Then the Chief Weasel began to sing in a high, squeaky voice:

> "Toad he went a-pleasuring
> Gaily down the street—"

The Badger drew himself up, took a firm grip of his stick with both paws, glanced around at his comrades, and cried, "The hour is come! Follow me!" And he flung the door open wide.

What a squealing and a squeaking and a screeching filled the air! Well might the terrified weasels dive under the tables and spring madly up at the windows! Well might the ferrets rush wildly for the fireplace and get hopelessly jammed in the chimney!

Glass and china went crashing to the floor as tables and chairs were flung aside in the panic of that terrible moment when the four Heroes strode boldly into the room! The mighty Badger's stick whistled through the air. The Mole, black and grim, waved his stick and shouted his awful war cry, "A Mole! A Mole!" Rat ran about, desperate and determined, his belt bulging with weapons of every variety. The Toad, frenzied with excitement and injured pride, swollen to twice his ordinary size, leaped into the air, emitting Toad-whoops that chilled them to the bone!

"Toad he went a-pleasuring!" he yelled. "*I'll* pleasure 'em!" And he went straight for the Chief Weasel.

They were but four in all, but to the panic-stricken weasels the hall seemed full of monstrous animals—gray, black, brown, and yellow, whooping and swinging enormous clubs. The weasels fled with squeals of terror, this way and that, through the windows, up the chimney—anywhere to get out of reach of those terrible sticks.

The affair was soon over. Up and down the whole length of the hall strode the four friends, whacking with their sticks at every head that showed itself. In five minutes the room was cleared. Through the broken windows came the shrieks of terrified weasels escaping across the lawn. Mole was busy handcuffing a dozen or so of the enemy lying on the floor.

The Badger, resting from his labors, leaned on his stick and wiped his honest brow. "Mole," he said, "you're the best of fellows! Run outside and see what those stoat-sentries are doing. I've an idea that, thanks to you, we won't have much trouble with *them* tonight!"

The Mole promptly vanished through a window. The Badger asked the other two to set a table on its legs again, pick up knives, forks, plates, and glasses, and see if they could rustle up some food. "I want some grub, I do," he said, in that rather common way he had of speaking. "Look lively, Toad! We've got your house back for you, and you don't offer us so much as a sandwich."

Toad felt rather hurt that the Badger didn't compliment him, as he had the Mole, and tell him what a fine fellow he was, and how splendidly he had fought. For Toad was particularly pleased with himself and the way he had gone for the Chief Weasel and sent him flying across the table with one blow of his stick. But he bustled about, and so did the Rat, and they soon found some jelly, a cold chicken, lobster salad, a basket of rolls, and plenty of cheese, butter, and celery.

They were just about to sit down when the Mole climbed in through a window, chuckling, with an armful of rifles. "It's all over," he reported. "As soon as the stoats, who were already very nervous and jumpy, heard the shrieks and uproar inside the hall, some of them threw down their rifles and fled.

"When the weasels came rushing out toward the other stoats, they thought they were betrayed, and the stoats grappled with the weasels, and the weasels fought to get away, and they wrestled and punched each other, and rolled over and over, until they fell into the river! They've all disappeared by now, and I've got their rifles."

"Excellent and deserving animal!" said the Badger, his mouth full of chicken and salad. "Now, there's just one more thing I want you to do, Mole, before you sit down to supper. I wouldn't trouble you if I didn't trust you the most. I want you to take those weasels on the floor there upstairs with you, and have them clean and tidy the bedrooms. See that they put clean sheets and pillow cases on. And then you can give them a licking apiece, if it's any satisfaction to you, and put them out by the back door."

The good-natured Mole picked up a stick, lined up his prisoners, gave them the order "Quick march!" and led his squad off to the upper floor. After a while, he reappeared smiling and said that every room was as clean as a new pin. "And I didn't have to lick them either," he added. "The weasels said they were extremely sorry for what they had done, but it was all the fault of the Chief Weasel and the stoats, and if ever they could do anything to make up for it, we had only to call them. So I gave them a roll apiece, and let them out at the back, and off they ran as hard as they could!"

Then the Mole pulled a chair up to the table and pitched into the cold chicken. Toad, like the gentleman he was, put all his jealousy behind him and said heartily, "Thank you kindly, dear Mole, for all your pains and trouble tonight, and especially for your cleverness this morning!"

The Badger was pleased at that and said, "There spoke my brave Toad!"

So they finished their supper in great joy and contentment, and presently retired to rest between clean sheets, safe in Toad's ancestral home, won back by matchless valor, clever strategy, and a proper handling of sticks.

The following morning, Toad, who had overslept as usual, came down to breakfast disgracefully late. He found on the table a pile of eggshells, some fragments of cold toast, a coffeepot three-fourths empty, and little else. This did not sit well with him, considering that, after all, it was his own house. Through the French windows of the breakfast room he could see the Mole and the Water Rat sitting in wicker chairs out on the lawn, evidently telling each other stories, roaring with laughter and kicking their short legs up in the air.

The Badger, who was in an armchair reading the morning paper, had merely looked up and nodded when Toad entered the room. But Toad knew his man, so he sat down and made the best breakfast he could, merely observing to himself that he would get square with the others sooner or later.

When he was nearly finished, the Badger looked up and remarked abruptly, "I'm sorry, Toad, but I'm afraid there's a heavy morning's work ahead of you. You see, we really ought to have a Banquet at once, to celebrate this affair. It's expected of you—in fact, it's the rule."

"Oh, all right!" the Toad said readily. "Anything to oblige. Though why on earth you would want to have a Banquet in the morning I cannot understand."

"Don't pretend to be stupider than you really are," replied the Badger crossly. "What I mean is, the Banquet will be at night, of course, but the invitations will have to be written and got off at once, and you've got to write 'em. Now sit down at that table—there's stacks of letter paper on it—and write invitations to all our friends. If you stick to it we shall get them out before luncheon."

"What!" cried Toad, dismayed. "Me stay indoors and write a lot of rotten letters on a sunny morning like this, when I want to go around my property, and put everything in order, and swagger about and enjoy myself! Certainly not!" He paused, struck by a sudden thought. Then he said, "Why, of course, dear Badger! You wish it done, and it shall be done. Go, Badger, order the Banquet, order what you like. I'll sacrifice this fair morning out of duty and friendship."

The Badger looked at him very suspiciously, but Toad's frank, open expression made it difficult to suggest any unworthy reason for his change of attitude. He left the room, and as soon as the door had closed, Toad hurried to the writing table. He *would* write the invitations, and he would take care to mention the leading part he had taken in the fight—how he had laid the Chief Weasel flat. He would hint at his adventures, and what a career of triumph he had to tell about. He would also outline a program of entertainment, including a speech by Toad on various subjects, a song composed by Toad, and other compositions written and sung by Toad.

He worked very hard and got all the letters finished by noon, at which hour a small weasel rang the doorbell, inquiring timidly whether he might be of any service. Toad shoved the bundle of invitations into his paw and told him to run along quick and deliver them, and there might be a shilling for him when he returned.

When the other animals came back to luncheon, after a morning on the river, the Mole, whose conscience had been pricking him, looked doubtfully at Toad, expecting to find him sulky. Instead, he was so high in spirits that the Mole began to suspect something. The Rat and the Badger exchanged suspicious glances.

As soon as the meal was over, Toad started off, but the Rat caught him by the arm. "Now, look here, Toad," he said. "It's about this Banquet, and very sorry I am to have to speak to you like this. But we want you to understand clearly that there are going to be no speeches and no songs."

Toad's pleasant dream was shattered. "Mayn't I sing them just one *little* song?" he pleaded piteously.

"No, not *one* little song," replied the Rat firmly, though his heart bled as he noticed the trembling lip of the poor, disappointed Toad. "You know well that your songs are full of boasting and self-praise. You *must* turn over a new leaf sooner or later, and now seems a splendid time to begin."

Toad remained a long while plunged in thought. At last he raised his head, and traces of strong emotion were visible on his face. "You are right, I know, and I was wrong. Henceforth I will be a very different Toad. My friends, you will never have occasion to blush for me again. But, oh dear, oh dear, this is a hard world!"

Pressing a handkerchief to his face, Toad left the room with shaky steps.

"The thing had to be done," Badger said gloomily. "The good fellow has got to live here and be respected, not mocked and laughed at by stoats and weasels."

"Speaking of weasels," said the Rat, "it's lucky we came upon that little weasel, just as he was setting out with Toad's invitations. They were simply disgraceful. I got rid of them, and the good Mole has volunteered to prepare simple invitation cards."

At last the hour for the Banquet drew near, and Toad, who on leaving the others had retired to his bedroom, was still sitting there, sad and thoughtful. Gradually his face cleared, and he began to smile. Then he took to giggling in a shy, self-conscious manner. At last he got up, locked the door, drew the curtains closed, collected all the chairs in the room, and took up his position in front of them, swelling visibly. Then he bowed and lifted his voice in song to an imaginary audience.

Toad's Last Little Song!

The Toad—came—home!
There was panic in the parlor and howling in the hall,
There was crying in the cowshed and shrieking in the
    stall,
When the Toad—came—home!

When the Toad—came—home!
There was smashing in of window and crashing in of
    door,
There was chasing of weasels that fainted on the floor,
When the Toad—came—home!

Bang! go the drums!
The trumpeters are tooting and the soldiers are
    saluting,
And the cannon they are shooting and the motorcars
    are hooting.
As the—Hero—comes!

Shout—Hooray!
And let each one of the crowd try and shout it very
    loud,
In honor of an animal of whom you're justly proud.
For it's Toad's—great—day!

He sang this very loud, and when he had done, he sang it all over again. Then he heaved a deep sigh—a long, long, long sigh.

Then he dipped his hairbrush in the water jug, parted his hair in the middle, and plastered it down very straight. He unlocked the door and went quietly down the stairs to greet his guests, who he knew must be assembling in the drawing room.

All the animals cheered when he entered, and crowded around to congratulate him and say nice things about his courage, and his cleverness, and his fighting qualities. But the Toad only smiled faintly and murmured, "Not at all!" Or, sometimes for a change, "On the contrary!"

Otter, who was standing at the hearthrug, describing to an admiring circle of friends exactly how he would have managed things had he been there, came forward with a shout and threw his arms around Toad's neck. He tried to march Toad around the room in triumph, but Toad disengaged himself, remarking gently, "Badger was the mastermind. The Mole and the Water Rat did most of the fighting. I merely served in the ranks and did little or nothing."

The animals were evidently puzzled and surprised by Toad's unexpected attitude. And Toad felt, as he moved from one guest to the other, making his modest responses, that he was an object of intense interest to everyone.

The Badger had ordered the best of everything, and the Banquet was a great success. There was much talking and laughter and joking among the animals. But Toad only looked down his nose and murmured pleasant remarks to the animals on either side of him. Occasionally he stole a glance at the Badger and the Rat, who stared at each other with their mouths open. This gave Toad the greatest satisfaction.

As the evening wore on, some of the livelier animals whispered to each other that things were not so amusing as they used to be in the good old days. There were some knockings on the tables and cries of "Toad! Speech! Speech from Toad! Song! Mr. Toad's Song!"

But Toad only shook his head gently and raised a paw in mild protest.

He was indeed an altered Toad!

After this, the four animals continued to lead their lives in joy and contentment. Toad, after due consultation with his friends, selected a handsome gold chain and locket set with pearls, which he sent to the jailer's daughter with a letter that even the Badger admitted to be modest, grateful, and appreciative. The engine driver, in his turn, was properly thanked and compensated for all his pains.

Even the bargewoman was, with some trouble, sought out. The value of her horse was made good to her. Toad kicked terribly at this, but the amount involved turned out to be approximately that at which the gypsy had valued it.

Sometimes, in the course of long summer evenings, the friends would take a stroll together in the Wild Wood. As far as they were concerned, it was now properly tamed. And it was pleasing to see how respectfully they were greeted by the inhabitants. As they passed through the wood, mother weasels would bring their young ones to the mouths of their holes, pointing in awe and whispering their praises.